TOP HAT

Stack no. 4 – Railway Tug

Only Star Tug v
raised wheelho
Tries to avoid a
dirty work.

WARRIOR

Stack no. 5 – Harbour Tug

Very strong, but sometimes clumsy. Will tackle any job.

HERCULES

Stack no. 6 – Ocean-going Tug

One of the leaders of the fleet. Very proud and rather aloof.

SUNSHINE

Stack no. 7 – Harbour Switcher

Newest member of the Star Fleet. Works mainly with Ten Cents.

TITLES AVAILABLE IN BUZZ BOOKS

THOMAS THE TANK ENGINE

1 Thomas in trouble
2 Toby and the Stout Gentleman
3 Percy runs away
4 Thomas and the Breakdown Train
5 Edward, Gordon and Henry
6 Thomas goes Fishing
7 Thomas down the Mine
8 James and the Troublesome Trucks
9 Gordon off the Rails
10 Thomas and Terence
11 James and the Tar Wagons
12 Thomas and Bertie
13 Thomas and the Trucks
14 Thomas's Christmas Party

FIREMAN SAM

1 Trevor's Trial Run
2 Norman's Spooky Night
3 A Bad Day for Dilys
4 Bella and the Bird's Nest
5 The Pride of Pontypandy
6 A Surprise for Sarah
7 Elvis's Experiment
8 Christmas in Pontypandy

TUGS

1 Kidnapped
2 Run Aground
3 Nothing to Declare
4 Treasure Hunt

BUGS BUNNY

1 Ali Baba Bunny
2 Knighty Knight Bugs
3 Broomstick Bunny
4 Mutiny on the Bunny

BARNEY

1 Barney and the Picnic
2 Barney's New Hair-Do
3 Barney Goes Shopping
4 Barney's Happy Christmas

MICRO MACHINES

1 Road Block
2 Hijack
3 Safe Breakers
4 Snowbound

GREMLINS

1 Don't Get Wet
2 Midnight Feast

First published 1990 by Buzz Books,
an imprint of the Octopus Publishing Group,
Michelin House, 81 Fulham Road, London, SW3 6RB.

LONDON MELBOURNE AUCKLAND

Story by Fiona Hardwick
Illustrations by The County Studio
Based on the television series TUGS produced by TUGS Ltd
for Clearwater Features (1986) Ltd and TVS Television,

ISBN 1 85591 014 4

Printed and bound in the UK by BPCC Paulton Books Ltd.

A TUGS ADVENTURE

NOTHING TO DECLARE

Story by Fiona Hardwick

Illustrations by The County Studio

Bigg City Port was bustling as usual. Warrior was busy with Lord Stinker, cleaning up the rubbish and Big Mac was unloading a cargo freighter.

Captain Star, the owner of Star Pier, was giving orders and keeping an eye on everyone in the harbour.

WARRIOR

"Keep to it, Star Tugs. Bluenose, the Naval Tug, is coming at midday to check we're all present and correct!"

"Oh no, not that pompous Bluenose," complained Top Hat. "Why is he coming?"

"It's a security check," said O.J. "Two new top secret Navy vessels are being docked here for a couple of days, so he's doing an inspection before they arrive."

O.J. always knew what was going on.

Out in the estuary, the Customs Launch saw a scruffy old freighter he recognised. An old enemy.

"Ahoy there, Johnny Cuba," said the launch sternly. "I'm coming aboard – just a routine search!"

Johnny Cuba was notorious for his smuggling, and Customs kept a close watch on him.

"Go ahead. I've got nothing to declare!"

"You always say that," muttered the Customs Launch as he came alongside.

SUNSHINE

But the launch could find nothing wrong.

"So tell your friends I can have a tow, right?" sneered Johnny. "Make it snappy – I get fed up, stuck here for hours!"

The launch noticed Sunshine nearby.

"Can you give Johnny a tow, Sunshine?"

"That's tricky. We're all busy preparing for Bluenose's inspection before those new ships arrive . . ."

"Yes, yes," interrupted the launch crossly. The whole operation was top secret and now Sunshine had given it away.

Johnny grinned slyly at this news.

"I suppose you thought you'd find spies on board when you searched me," he said, sniggering.

The launch glared at Sunshine and turned sharply back towards the harbour.

Johnny turned to face Sunshine.

"Now, if you want to keep your stack intact, don't forget to tell your little pals about my tow!"

Sunshine was not going to be bullied.

"You'll get a tow when one of us is free, and not before," he said defiantly, and set off for Star Pier.

Soon Johnny saw Big Mac coming towards him.

"You took your time," said Johnny rudely. "Get me towed in right now!"

"I'm on another job," grunted Big Mac. "One of the others will be here soon."

Johnny scowled.

Later, O.J. came puffing and wheezing up the estuary. With all the extra work, he was tired and hot.

"Come on old timer," called Johnny, "or would you like *me* to give *you* a tow?"

"I haven't got time for your stupid jokes," snapped O.J.

Then Ten Cents went by.

"Sunshine told me you need a tow. I'll be back in a few minutes when I finish this delivery," he called.

"Oh, don't worry about me," said Johnny. "I'm just watching myself go rusty!"

"Bunch of goody-goodies," he muttered. "Maybe the Z Stacks will be more useful."

So, when Zip appeared, Johnny yelled:

"Oi, you there! Give me a tow!"

"I'm . . . I'm too busy Johnny – um, ask Zorran," said Zip in a frightened voice.

Johnny watched Zip move out of sight.

"I give up!" he said. "I could be here all day. I might as well get some sleep."

He dozed off.

As he slept, a long grey craft appeared on the horizon, heading towards Bigg City Port.

A sudden noise made Johnny wake up.

"I suppose that's Bluenose – hey, what's that?" he said, catching sight of the strange shape approaching.

As he watched, it disappeared, leaving only bubbles on the surface of the water. A submarine – but what was it doing on its way to the harbour?

Johnny frowned. Bluenose's inspection was in preparation for top secret navy vessels. Perhaps the sub was to let everyone know the ships were on their way. But Johnny couldn't understand why it had suddenly disappeared.

He stared at where the sub had been – you'd never guess there had been anything there at all.

Then Johnny realised.

"It's a spy! Someone wants to know what these new ships are like, so they've sent in a spy. And with the Customs Launch and Bluenose at the inspection, there's no-one to stop it – except me!"

In those days, only large liners like the Duchess had radios, so Johnny couldn't tell anyone else what was going on.

Patiently, he waited for the sub to resurface.

Meanwhile, in the harbour, Bluenose was about to begin his inspection.

"The new ships are most, I said most, important. Top security is vital – absolutely tip top. Discipline – that's what the Navy is used to and that's what we expect!"

"Yes, Bluenose, of course, Bluenose," sighed Captain Star.

Bluenose made a thorough inspection. He looked inside every warehouse, checked all the barges and even wanted to have Warrior searched!

"Blinking cheek!" said Warrior.

Eventually, Bluenose was satisfied.

The Customs Launch got away as soon as he could.

Back in the estuary, the submarine had reappeared, and Johnny seized his chance.

He revved up his engines and rammed the sub as hard as he could, driving it on to some sandbanks.

Then the Customs Launch came past.

"Ahoy there, mate," called Johnny. "Come and take a look here. This sub is a long way from home and *very* interested in Bluenose's ships, I reckon."

A little later, Bluenose steamed by.

"That's right laddie," he said, when he saw the launch talking to Johnny Cuba. "Keep those ne'er do wells under control. Bit of discipline, that's what they need – make 'em tow the line!"

Bluenose laughed loudly at his own joke.

Johnny and the Customs Launch grinned.

"I never thought I'd say it, but thanks Johnny," said the launch. "Bluenose would never believe it, even if I told him!"

"No problem," said Johnny. "There's only room for one scoundrel round here – me! Now, where *is* my tow?"

THE Z STACKS

ZORRAN
Stack no. 1 – Harbour Tug
Leader of the Z Stacks. A mean, tough character.

ZEBEDEE
Stack no. 2 – Harbour Tug

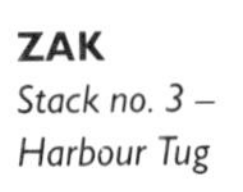

ZAK
Stack no. 3 – Harbour Tug